WE BOTH READ®

Parent's Introduction

Whether your child is a beginning reader, a reluctant reader, or an eager reader, this book offers a fun and easy way to encourage and help your child in reading.

Developed with reading education specialists, **We Both Read** books invite you and your child to take turns reading aloud. You read the left-hand pages of the book, and your child reads the right-hand pages—which have been written at one of six early reading levels. The result is a wonderful new reading experience and faster reading development!

You may find it helpful to read the entire book aloud yourself the first time, then invite your child to participate the second time. As you read, try to make the story come alive by reading with expression. This will help to model good fluency. It will also be helpful to stop at various points to discuss what you are reading. This will help increase your child's understanding of what is being read.

In some books, a few challenging words are introduced in the parent's text, distinguished with bold lettering. Pointing out and discussing these words can help to build your child's reading vocabulary. If your child is a beginning reader, it may be helpful to run a finger under the text as each of you reads. Please also notice that a "talking parent" ☺ icon precedes the parent's text, and a "talking child" ☺ icon precedes the child's text.

If your child struggles with a word, you can encourage "sounding it out," but keep in mind that not all words can be sounded out. Your child might pick up clues about a word from the picture, other words in the sentence, or any rhyming patterns. If your child struggles with a word for more than five seconds, it is usually best to simply say the word.

Most of all, remember to praise your child's efforts and keep the reading fun. After you have finished the book, ask a few questions and discuss what you have read together. Rereading this book multiple times may also be helpful for your child.

Try to keep the tips above in mind as you read together, but don't worry about doing everything right. Simply sharing the enjoyment of reading together will help increase your child's interest and skills in reading.

Baseball Fever

A We Both Read® Book

We Both Read® is a trademark of Treasure Bay, Inc.

Published by
Treasure Bay, Inc.
P.O. Box 119
Novato, CA 94948 USA

Printed in Malaysia

Library of Congress Catalog Card Number: 2002094713

ISBN: 978-1-891327-46-9

Visit us online at:
www.TreasureBayBooks.com

PR-10-17

WE BOTH READ®

Baseball Fever

By Sindy McKay

Illustrated by Meredith Johnson

TREASURE BAY

The clock in my classroom moved slowly toward three o'clock. It **always** moved slowly on baseball practice days. BBRRRIIIING! The last bell finally rang. I grabbed my backpack and raced toward the field as fast as I could!

I was going to be the first one there. I was almost **always** the first one there, but not today.

⊂◯   Karen Washington, the best shortstop around, got there before me. She waved and yelled, "Hi Jason!"

I answered her with a great big sneeze!

"Whoa, are you okay?" she asked.

I told her I was fine. Then I ran to the **pitcher's** mound to get in some practice before **Coach** Bill arrived.

Coach Bill was a great coach. He made our team a great team. He made me a great **pitcher**!

Coach Bill sent four of us to the outfield while the rest of the team lined up for batting practice. Karen stepped up and hit a high fly, right to me.

"I've got it!" I called as I moved under the ball. Then I **sneezed**.

I **sneezed** hard. Then I sneezed again—and again.

The ball hit the dirt at my feet.

Coach Bill ran out to see if I was okay.

"Looks like you're getting sick, Jason," he said. "You better go home and take care of yourself. Saturday is our first game of the season, and I don't want you to miss it!"

I didn't want to go home, but Coach Bill
said I had to.

I didn't want to be sick, but I was.

That night at dinner, Mom noticed I wasn't eating my peas. I love peas—but they tasted kind of yucky tonight. Mom frowned and reached across the table to feel my forehead. "Do you feel okay?" she asked.

"I feel fine," I said. "I feel great!" Then I
sneezed again.

Mom sent me right to bed.

When I woke up the next morning I didn't feel so good. My throat was scratchy and my nose was stuffy, and I didn't really feel like going to school or to **baseball practice** or anything. I just wanted to crawl under my covers and go back to sleep.

Mom came in my room. I told her I felt great!
"I can't wait to go to school," I said. "I can't
wait to go to **baseball practice**."

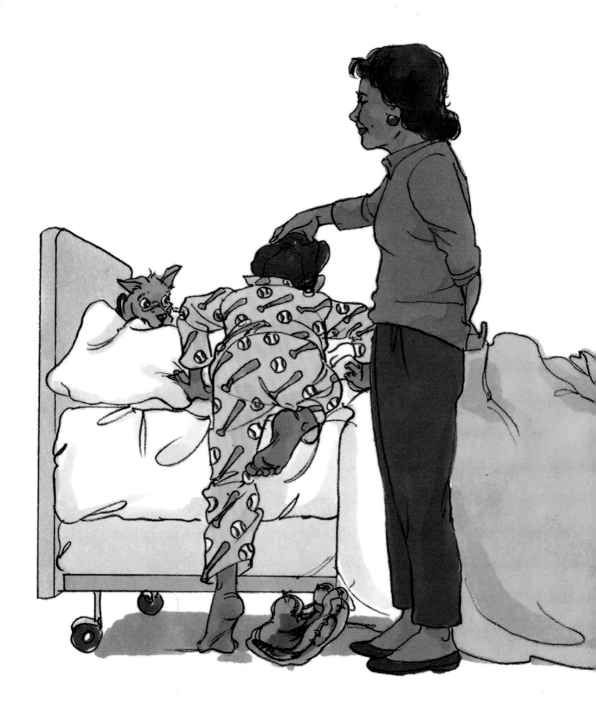

Mom said I looked miserable. She informed me there would
be no school this morning and there would definitely be no
baseball practice this afternoon.

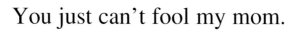 You just can't fool my mom.

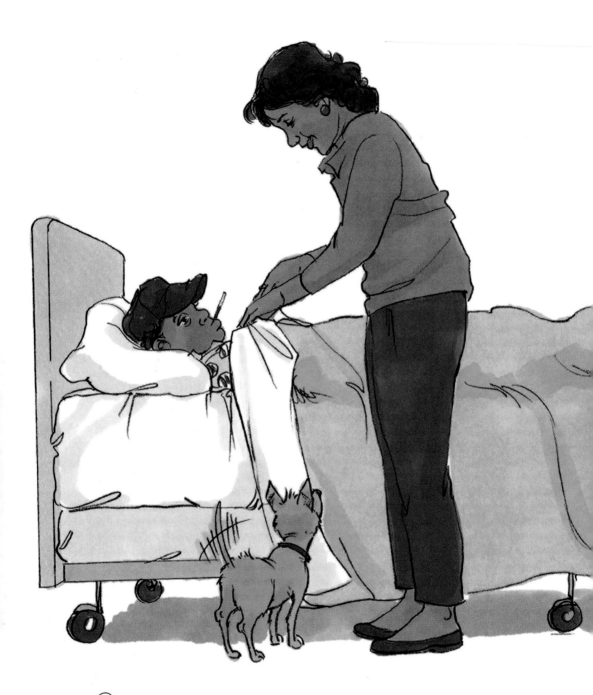

Mom tucked me back under the covers and took my temperature.

"You have a little **fever**," she said. "I'll get you some medicine. You try to get some rest."

I didn't want to have a **fever**. So I got some rest.

When I woke up, I told Mom I felt great! But

she still didn't let me go to baseball practice.

That evening Karen Washington called.

"We missed you today," she said. "Tim Anderson is working on his **fastball,** but he hasn't quite mastered the grip yet. I hope you feel better in time for the game on Saturday."

It felt good to know they missed me. It felt good to know they missed my **fastball**.

I just had to get well in time for the game!

I tried to go to sleep early that night. But every time I laid my head down, I started to cough. Mom said if I didn't feel better in the **morning**, she'd take me to see the **doctor**. I finally fell asleep and had a great dream about pitching a no-hitter in front of a big crowd!

The next **morning** I felt great! Then I got out
of bed. I didn't feel so great anymore.

Mom took me to see the **doctor**.

We arrived at Dr. Elman's office and waited until the nurse came out and called my name. She took us back into an examination room and asked me some questions, then took my **temperature** with a really cool-looking thermometer.

She put it in my ear and waited until it went "beep." Then she took it out and smiled.

"Your **temperature** is good," she said.

She told us Dr. Elman would be in to see us in just a few minutes, then left.

While we waited, I explored the exam room. There were lots of cabinets and a sink with a funny faucet you could turn on by pressing petals with your feet. And there were **posters** on the walls.

One **poster** was about food. Another poster
showed where the food goes in your body. The
biggest poster was the best one I had ever seen.

"That's Cy Young, the greatest pitcher that ever lived."

I turned around to find **Dr. Elman** standing in the doorway, grinning.

"I just got that poster last week," he continued. "You like it?"

"Like it?" I said. "I LOVE it! I'm a pitcher too, you know."

Dr. Elman smiled. "Yes, I know."

27

 I smiled back and told him that was why he had to make me better today. "I just have to pitch in the first game of the season tomorrow!"

Dr. Elman said he couldn't make any promises, but he would do his best. Then he started the examination.

He looked in my ears. He looked in my eyes. He looked at my throat. He felt my neck. He even looked up my nose!

Then he listened to my heart and told me to take deep breaths while he listened to my lungs.

"What do you hear?" I asked anxiously. "Will I be okay by **tomorrow**?"

"Hmmm . . . I think I hear the roar of the crowd at a baseball game," he answered with a grin.

"Does that mean I can play **tomorrow**?"

Dr. Elman shook his head. "I'm sorry, Jason," he said. "You will be fine, but not by tomorrow."

He told my mother that it didn't look like anything serious, but I should stay in bed over the weekend. Then he turned to me and said, "I wish I knew of some way to get you better in time for the game tomorrow, but I'm afraid there's still no cure for the common cold."

He did wish he could help me. I could tell.

"It's okay, Dr. Elman," I told him. "It's just a game."

Then Mom and I went home.

Saturday morning I woke up feeling pretty sick. I also felt really sad about missing the first game of the season. Then I heard the **phone** ring. After a moment, I heard my mom's **voice** calling up to me in my room.

 "It's for you, Jason," Mom said.

She gave me the **phone**, and I said, "Hello?"

"Hi, Jason," said a **voice**. "It's Karen!"

Karen Washington was calling me from the baseball field! "We're still in the first **inning** of the game," she reported. "Tim Anderson is pitching and he's doing great! We tagged a runner out on first and Dan caught a fly ball and Tim actually struck somebody out!"

"I have to go now," she said. "Coach Bill says I'm up next! I'll call you back next **inning**."

It was fantastic! Every inning someone on the team called me to fill me in on what was happening. It wasn't quite as good as being there in person, but it was **really** close. Even my mom wanted to hear the next report!

Our team played **really** well. The other team also played well, but we must have played better because we won the game!

Mom said she was really sorry I couldn't be there to celebrate with my friends.

"It's okay," I said. "There will be lots of other games."

Playing ball is really fun. So is winning. But the very best part of baseball is having such good, good friends.

If you liked *Baseball Fever,* here are some other
We Both Read® books you are sure to enjoy!

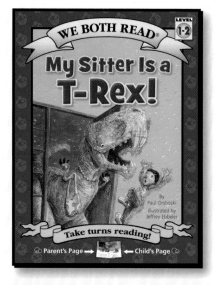

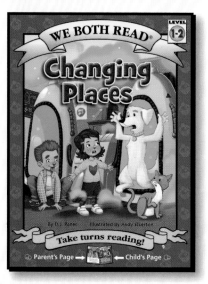

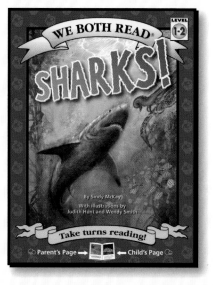

To see all the We Both Read books that are available,
just go online to **www.WeBothRead.com**.